G7 9|17
11/1/18
12/11/21
4/11/22

Return this item by the last date shown.
Items may be renewed by telephone or at
www.ercultureandleisure.org/libraries

east renfrewshire
CULTURE
and LEISURE

Barrhead:	0141 577 3518	Mearns:	0141 577 4979
Busby:	0141 577 4971	Neilston:	0141 577 4981
Clarkston:	0141 577 4972	Netherlee:	0141 637 5102
Eaglesham:	0141 577 3932	Thornliebank:	0141 577 4983
Giffnock:	0141 577 4976	Uplawmoor:	01505 850564

Raintree is an imprint of Capstone Global Library Limited, a company
incorporated in England and Wales having its registered office at
264 Banbury Road, Oxford, OX2 7DY – Registered company number: 6695582

www.raintree.co.uk
myorders@raintree.co.uk

Edited by Eliza Leahy
Designed by Tracy McCabe
Original illustrations © Capstone 2017
Illustrated by Xavier Bonet
Image Credits: Shutterstock: Dmitry Natashin, black box design element
Production by Kathy McColley
Printed and bound in China.

ISBN 978 1 4747 4419 5
21 20 19 18 17
10 9 8 7 6 5 4 3 2 1

British Library Cataloguing in Publication Data
A full catalogue record for this book is available from the British
Library.

Acknowledgements
Every effort has been made to contact copyright holders of material
reproduced in this book. Any omissions will be rectified in subsequent
printings if notice is given to the publisher.

All the internet addresses (URLs) given in this book were valid at
the time of going to press. However, due to the dynamic nature of the
internet, some addresses may have changed, or sites may have changed or
ceased to exist since publication. While the author and publisher regret
any inconvenience this may cause readers, no responsibility for any such
changes can be accepted by either the author or the publisher.

THE GIRL IN THE GRAVEYARD

AND OTHER SCARY TALES

By Michael Dahl

Illustrated by
Xavier Bonet

raintree

a Capstone company — publishers for children

CONTENTS

Dear Reader,

When I was 10 years old, I considered myself an expert on fear. I read a library book that described many phobias.

Astraphobia, fear of lightning and thunder
Coulrophobia, fear of clowns
Pithecophobia, fear of monkeys
Plasmophobia, fear of ghosts
Spheksophobia, fear of wasps

Yup, I had those fears for sure. And more.

A very common fear is monophobia, the fear of being alone. I have this fear too.

That's one reason I like reading. I'm never alone if I have a book. When I read, I feel as though I'm listening to someone talking to me, right there by my side.

The stories in this book are all about people with special fears.

But a word of advice: Once you've finished reading them, forget all about them.

The library book warned that if you think about other people's fears too much, they have a strange tendency to become your own ...

Michael Dahl

LITTLE IMPS

"Isabel, hurry up! I need to use the bathroom!" Hattie pounded on the door as she shouted to her sister inside. "Pleeeeeeeease!"

Her older sister, Isabel, did not answer.

"I can hear you in there," called Hattie. "Just let me in for a second."

Still no answer.

"You are just rude!" said Hattie. "You're an imp." She felt powerful saying the word her elderly neighbour, Mr Slater, had used when describing some noisy neighbourhood children. "A big, fat imp!"

"Who are you calling an imp, imp?" asked

Isabel. The older girl appeared at the other end of the hallway, still in her pyjamas and rubbing her eyes as she stepped out of her bedroom. Hattie's jaw dropped open.

"But Isabel," said Hattie, "you're in the bathroom."

Isabel yawned. "Really? Then why am I standing over here?" she asked.

Hattie turned back to the bathroom door, confused.

Isabel walked down the hallway and stopped at Hattie's side. "You're obviously wrong," she said. "I'm right here. Mum must be in there." Isabel pounded on the door. "Mum, let us in."

A familiar voice called from the kitchen at the other end of the house. "You two need to get ready for school. It's getting late. And stop with all the yelling!" she yelled.

The sisters stared at each other. Who was in the bathroom if it wasn't their mum? Isabel grabbed the door handle.

"It's locked," Hattie pointed out.

Isabel rattled the handle. "No, it's just stuck."

The older girl made a fierce turn of the handle, then shoved the door open.

Once inside, the two girls froze. Wet towels covered the floor. One was draped over – and into – the toilet. Water was running in the sink. Toothpaste had been squeezed onto the walls. Talcum powder was sprinkled on the floor and over the surfaces.

"Who made this mess?" asked Isabel.

"I thought it was you," said Hattie.

"Not me," she said. Isabel pointed to the mirror.

Hattie stood next to her sister and peered into the mirror over the sink. They could see the rest of the room reflected in its shiny surface. But there was something else. The cupboard door was moving. Hattie turned around quickly. The real cupboard door, the one between them and the bathtub, was shut, like it normally was. In the mirror, however, the door was slowly opening.

As Hattie stared into the mirror, she saw a small creature, with pink, scaly skin and yellow cat's eyes, peek around the cupboard door.

Talcum powder covered the creature's skin. Toothpaste was smeared over its dark red lips. The creature widened its toothy smile and then stuck out its tongue at Hattie.

"How rude!" said Hattie. "Did you see that?" she asked her sister.

But Isabel had gone. A flash of pink caught Hattie's eye. She glanced back at the mirror and saw her sister being pulled into the mirror's cupboard by the little scaly creature. When she looked back at the real cupboard behind her, it was normal. Hattie turned to the mirror and saw the creature had been joined by two others, all of them grinning with rows and rows of sharp, tiny teeth.

"Hattie, help!" screamed Isabel. The cupboard in the mirror slammed shut.

Hattie turned to look at the real cupboard. She ran and opened it. The space was full of shelves and towels and bottles of soap. There was no room for a person to stand inside, let alone four creatures.

Hattie ran to her bedroom and shut the door. She collapsed onto her bed and sobbed. It was a dream. It had to be. How could Isabel disappear inside a mirror? What were those horrible little things with the yellow eyes and the cruel smiles?

Hattie heard a creak.

She lifted her wet eyes from her pillow and watched as the cupboard door across her bedroom slowly opened. A scaly pink hand reached around the edge of the door. It was followed by a familiar looking face.

Isabel?

The strange creature looked like Hattie's sister, but with pink, scaly skin and yellow eyes. She looked at Hattie, opened her toothy mouth and said, "Your turn, Hattie. You can come in now".

NIGHT OF THE FALLING STAR

"**Y**ou can't come," said Eddie. "You're too young."

"I'm nine," said Ollie.

"That's too young," said Eddie. "Besides, meteors could be dangerous."

"It's not a meteor anymore," Ollie said. "When it hits the Earth, it's called a meteorite."

Their dad walked out onto the dark porch and asked why they were arguing. Eddie explained that a shooting star had landed outside town, and that all his friends were driving out to see it.

Ollie corrected him and said that a meteorite

had crashed out past Paul's Valley, and that Eddie refused to take him.

"Is that what the big boom was?" their father asked.

"It crashed just an hour ago," said Ollie. "And Eddie won't take me."

Their father looked at Eddie. "Take your brother."

"He'll get in the way," said Eddie.

"Take your brother," repeated their dad. "It'll be a fun outing for you two."

Eddie groaned.

"Yes!" said Ollie, pumping his fist.

* * *

Eddie was quiet during the drive, but Ollie was too excited to keep still. "I bet we'll get there before the scientists do," said Ollie. "It'll probably be too hot to touch. Of course, we might just see a big hole in the ground. The meteorite will be buried deep underground, right in the middle of things. I wonder if it's magnetic. Use your phone, Eddie. See if it's magnetic when we get there. Check your compass app. See if it goes wild like it does in the movies."

"Weird," said Eddie. It was the first time he had spoken in half an hour.

"What's weird, Eddie?" asked Ollie.

His brother pulled over onto the side of the road. The sun had set during their drive out. There weren't many lights this far out of town, but they could see at least twenty other vehicles parked along both sides of the highway.

"Nobody's around," said Eddie. "Pete said he was coming out."

"They're all looking at the meteorite," Ollie said.

"Somebody would be out here," said Eddie. "And it's so quiet."

Ollie had to admit that it was strangely silent. Especially if there were that many people from town together in one place.

"Well, come on," said Eddie. "Let's go and take a look."

It was easy to tell which way the meteorite had

landed. Clouds of thick vapour poured through the trees on the south side of the road.

At first, Eddie and Ollie had no trouble finding a path through the short grass and passing the row of trees. Grasshoppers leaped out of their way, disappearing into the dark. The further they went, the thicker the vapour became.

"I still can't hear anything," Eddie mumbled.

"We should have brought a torch," said Ollie.

Ahead, in the distance, a reddish glow burned through the vapour like another setting sun. "That's it!" yelled Ollie. He was about to run towards it, but his brother gripped his shoulder.

"Listen," said Eddie.

"I can't hear anything," said Ollie.

He realized that he couldn't even hear crickets. Then –

It was faint. Like a hundred people talking and shouting. It sounded as if the brothers were standing in the carpark outside a football stadium, and the cries of the crowd barely reached their ears.

The closer they got to the meteorite, thought Ollie, the louder the people from town should be.

Where were they?

Ollie and Eddie took a few more steps towards the glow. With each step, Ollie could hear the faraway cries again.

Ollie felt funny. His eyelids were heavy. His head ached. He took a few deep breaths. "I don't feel well, Eddie," he said.

"Yeah, I'm not feeling great either," said Eddie. "Maybe it's the mist. It's hard to breathe."

"I want to go back to the truck," said Ollie.

Eddie grabbed his arm and led him in the direction of the road. Ollie could feel the warmth from the meteorite against his back as they walked. He didn't regret not taking a closer look. He felt uneasy now, and he just wanted to go home.

"Where are the trees?" asked Eddie.

They had been walking for what seemed a long time. *Are we lost? What's with all this tall grass?* Ollie wondered. They hadn't walked through any of this tall grass on the way out. The grass waved high above their heads. It was growing! "Eddie!" cried Ollie.

"Don't worry," said his older brother. "Let's just keep going. I know this is the right way."

They kept floundering through the tall grass. Soon Ollie heard the sounds of engines roaring up ahead. The highway!

"Those sound like jet planes," mumbled Eddie.

Suddenly, the jungle of grass came to an end. There was a sharp straight line of grass that marked its outer edge. Next to the grass ran a border of dirt and then a mound of hard, black tar. "This must be the road," said Eddie. He kept walking. "We must have got lost in that grass and ended up away from the cars."

Ollie was a metre or two from the empty road when he hard a click behind him. He turned and saw a pale green snout push through the tall grass. It had eyes the size and colour of basketballs. Long feelers, like the antenna on Eddie's truck, wiggled at the top of its twitching head. The creature clicked and whirred. It scooted out of the grass with sickening speed.

"Eddie, help me!" screamed Ollie. He raced as fast as he could towards his brother. He heard the creature clicking behind him, coming closer.

When Ollie reached Eddie standing on the road, the creature stopped. The pale green head pivoted back and forth. Its long front legs twitched. With a spring, the creature flew high above them and disappeared back into the grass.

Ollie stood next to his brother on the highway. He couldn't speak. He wanted to say the word "grasshopper" but it refused to leave his dry, frightened mouth.

Now he knew why the grass was so tall. Why it appeared to be growing. Why they couldn't see the trees, and why the road looked so different from before. Everything was the same, except for them.

The grass hadn't been growing. They had been shrinking!

"It was the mist, Eddie," said Ollie. "Something in the mist."

"And that noise we heard," said Eddie. "Like people far away . . ."

With every step, they had heard distant cries. Cries of people yelling out in terror. In pain. Before they were crushed.

"Who's that?" said Eddie. "Is that Pete?"

Ollie heard the voice too. It did not come from below. This voice was loud, almost booming, and it came from up above.

He looked up and the sky disappeared. It was blotted out by the sole of an enormous shoe.

THE BABY MONITOR

Samantha Moore was helping her mother organize shelves in the basement when she found it. A small blue and pink box-like device sat on the top shelf. It had a dial; a thick, rubber antenna; and what looked like a small built-in speaker. "Is that a radio?" she asked.

Her mother glanced up and smiled. "That's your baby monitor," she said. "I haven't seen that for years."

"Does it still work?" asked Samantha.

Mrs Moore reached up and pulled down the device. "I suppose if you put batteries in it," she said, handing it to Sam.

Sam turned a dial on the side. A crackle of static burst from the speaker. "It *does* work," she cried.

Samantha's mother began opening other boxes. "It doesn't work without the other half," she pointed out. "That's just the receiver your father and I kept in our room. The actual baby monitor went in your room, right next to your bed. That's how we could hear what was going on."

Her mother tapped the device. "And that's the button we hit when we wanted to talk back to you. Sometimes you just wanted to hear my voice, then you'd go back to sleep."

Sam saw words on the back of the receiver: range: up to 30 metres. She grinned. Her best friend, Dawnay, lived less than fifteen metres from her in their crowded neighbourhood.

"We have to find it," said Samantha.

"That thing is so old," said her mum. Sam didn't care. Her parents had refused to get her a phone for at least another year. With the monitor, she and Dawnay could talk to each other whenever they wanted.

Samantha and her mother combed through all the boxes and the remaining shelves. They found Christmas decorations; wallpaper; a rusty, blocky machine called a typewriter; and lots of dead insects. But no baby monitor. Sam's mother said, "I'll look through my wardrobe later. I don't see why we would have thrown out the monitor. Especially as we kept the receiver."

By the time Samantha was ready for bed, her mother had still not found the missing half of the monitor. "Don't worry," she said. "We'll look again in the morning. I'm pretty sure it must be downstairs."

Samantha lay in her dark bedroom, dreaming of finding the monitor. She couldn't wait until she had it in her hand and ran next door to show Dawnay. Her friend would be so surprised!

"Samantha . . . ," someone said.

Sam sat up. "Mum?" she said quietly.

There was a crackle. Static. A small red light glowed on the baby monitor's receiver that sat on Sam's dresser. The voice was coming from its speaker.

"Sam . . ."

Samantha got out of bed and walked over to

the receiver. She hesitated before picking up the device. She pushed the button her mother had shown her earlier. "This . . . this is Sam," she said quietly into the speaker. "Who's this?"

Another crack of static. "Sam, it's me."

"Me who?" asked Sam.

"I'm here in the house," came the crackly voice.

A cold chill prickled the back of Samantha's neck. It was hard to tell if the voice belonged to a man or a woman. Or to an adult or child, for that matter.

The voice returned: "I have the other half of the baby monitor."

Well, of course. Whoever was talking must have found the rest of the device. And Sam wanted it. "Where are you?" asked Sam.

"Downstairs," came the voice. ". . . in the basement."

Sam pressed the button. "Come up and bring it with you."

There was a long pause. "It's too hard to climb the stairs, Sam."

The girl was getting colder the longer she stood barefoot by her dresser. "Just leave it on the basement steps," said Sam. "I'll get it in the morning."

The voice crackled. "Don't be afraid," it said. "You don't have to be afraid of me, Sam. I'm just a baby."

"Babies don't talk like that!" cried Sam.

"Some of us do," said the voice.

Sam stood there, not knowing what to do.

The voice returned. "Don't worry," it said. "You don't have to come down to the basement . . . I've come upstairs."

Sam heard a door creak open in the hallway. Her heart thumped in her chest. She needed to reach the front door and run from the house. She ran from her room, leaving the receiver behind.

Sam saw a small shadow at the other end of the hallway. A black mass the size of a grocery bag. And it was moving.

"See? I'm right here." This time Sam heard the voice clearer than before.

The small black shape moved into the dim light cast by the nightlight in the hallway. Sam shivered as she saw a small baby, standing, holding the baby monitor in its soft, flabby arms. The baby was hairless. Its face, dark blue, was partially hidden behind the monitor. It had sharp fingernails on its tiny fingers, of which Sam counted twelve.

"Here," said the baby. "Come and take it."

"Who – who are you?" said Sam.

The baby thing took a step closer. "I'm the baby monitor," it said. "I monitor all the babies. I look after them. Just like you have a lunch monitor at school. By the way, here we are on the landing. Do you have your pass, Samantha?" The baby cackled a hideous laugh. "Do you have your pass?" It raced towards the girl. Samantha heard a roar of wind and fainted onto the carpet.

* * *

The police were called the next morning. Samantha Moore's parents had found her bedroom empty, no doors or windows opened. She had disappeared overnight. It was on the news every evening for a month. During that time, helpful friends and neighbours brought over meals or helped clean the house. A few of them finished reorganizing the basement shelves. The old baby monitor receiver was packed in a box with other items to sell or give away. It sat in a far corner of the basement. At night, a faint crackling voice whispered from the receiver inside the box. It was muffled by the cardboard. But if someone stood close enough and put their ear next to the box they might have been able to hear. "Mum! Mum! Are you there? It's me, Samantha. I'm right here!" And sometimes, one could hear a baby laugh.

THE
HUNGRY
SNOWMAN

Arden pushed open the metal gate to the garden, sending half a dozen small icicles cascading off the bars and shattering onto the cold pavement below. He hitched his rucksack up on one shoulder, closed the gate behind him, and trudged further into the deep snow in the garden. His sister, Rosie, was there, wrapped up in scarves and mittens and a hat. She was doing something to the snowman he had built the day before.

"What are you doing?" asked Arden.

"I'm feeding him. He's hungry," said Rosie.

"He's not a living thing," said Arden. He had just been learning about biology during his science unit that day at school. He had memorized the three things that defined life. "It doesn't move, it doesn't breathe and it doesn't eat. It's not alive."

Rosie was patting the snowman's mouth. "Poor snowman hasn't eaten all day."

"What's that stuff on his face?" asked Arden. He peered closely at the snowman. "Is that birdseed?"

"I got it from the feeder," said Rosie.

"He looks like he's got freckles," said Arden. "Or measles."

"If the birds come to eat the birdseed," said Rosie. "Maybe the snowman will eat the birds."

"Gross!" said Arden.

"We eat birds," Rosie explained calmly. "Mum says we eat turkeys and chickens."

"Not me," said Arden. "From now on, I'm a vegetarian."

"What about chocolate peanut-butter cups?" the little girl asked. She knew those were her brother's favourite snack.

"Chocolate isn't meat," said Arden.

Rosie kept patting birdseed onto the snowman's face and humming. Arden was disgusted. He tromped out of the garden and into the house.

* * *

The next morning, on his way to the back gate, Arden stopped to glance at the snowman. He almost dropped his rucksack. He couldn't believe it. There were bird feathers stuck to the snowman's face. One actually poked out of the twigs and stones that made up his mouth.

Maybe the seed actually attracted some birds to the snowman, he thought. Arden suddenly felt as if he was going to lose his breakfast. Then the sick feeling turned into a small ball of anger. Why did Rosie do this? Why did she keep ruining his snowman? Arden lashed out and kicked it. He pushed the large snowballs that made up the figure's middle and head until they lay on the ground in a messy, snowy heap.

Arden turned. He saw Rosie watching him through the window. Arden just shook his head at her and headed towards the gate.

* * *

That afternoon, when Arden returned home and stepped through the garden gate, his anger returned. The snowman had been put back together. *Rosie must have been out here again,* he thought. Arden sighed, letting a puff of breath into the freezing air.

Arden trudged up to the snowman. Something was different. As the boy looked closer at the snowman's face, he grew angrier. Rosie had removed all the birdseed, but she had replaced it with something else. Chocolate peanut-butter cups ringed the snowman's mouth. *Arden's* peanut-butter cups! Ten of them. This was going too far.

Arden pulled off a glove and reached towards the chocolate treats stuck on the snowman's face. They were not going to stay out here, wasted in the cold. His attention was on the chocolate, but he should have looked more closely. He should have noticed the small drop of saliva that oozed out of the snowman's mouth. As the boy's bare fingers touched the first chocolate cup, it was too late.

The teeth felt like ice against his skin.

Rosie was inside the house, watching from a window. "The poor snowman *was* hungry," she said. As she closed the curtains and turned away from the window, the little girl frowned.

THE TALL AND SLENDER MAN

Charlotte walked into the kitchen. She saw that the back door stood wide open. But the square metal bolt of the lock was still sticking out. Still locked.

"**Y**ou shouldn't read those scary stories just before bed," said Charlotte's grandmother.

"I know, I know," said Charlotte, scrunched up on the sofa. She turned another page in the thick book on her lap. "Just one more," she said. "Then I'll go to bed, I promise."

Her grandmother smiled. The old woman turned to the dog at her side. "All right, Kenji. I'll let you out. Then it's off to bed for everyone."

The woman walked to the kitchen. Charlotte, who was deep in another scary story about the Tall Men, barely noticed the sound of the door opening and closing on Kenji. The series was one of Charlotte's favourites. The Tall Men would appear in different towns and cities across the world. Whenever someone saw them, walking slowly down a street, or standing in the shadows of a building, or climbing the stairs to someone's house, they knew something bad was going to happen. The Tall Men were omens. Messengers of doom.

"Will you let Kenji back in?" asked her grandmother.

"Of course." Charlotte nodded, her eyes glued to the page.

"I'm off to bed," said the old woman. She kissed her granddaughter on the forehead, and then trundled off to her bedroom at the back of the house. Charlotte's mother and father were already asleep upstairs.

Charlotte heard her grandmother call out. "Don't forget the dog!"

Charlotte put her book down and saw Kenji trotting towards the sofa. The dog was already inside. Kenji came up to her for an ear rub, but the girl stood up, ignoring him. How did the dog get back inside?

Charlotte walked into the kitchen. She saw that the back door stood wide open. But the square metal bolt of the lock was still sticking out. Still locked. Her grandmother always locked the doors, even for letting out Kenji. The older woman was afraid of thieves.

"Kenji, how did you get in?" said Charlotte quietly to herself. Kenji had followed her into the kitchen and had stopped beside her. But when Charlotte bent down to pet her, the dog had gone.

"Kenji?"

Charlotte looked behind her and watched as her dog stood up on his hind feet. A trick he had never done before. Taller and taller, the dog stretched up. His fur grew longer and became a long, thick, black coat. A coat with buttons and pockets and a collar. The man who was wearing the coat must have stood at least ten feet tall. He had to bend his head slightly so it wouldn't hit the ceiling.

"Where's Kenji?" Charlotte asked in a shaky voice.

"I thought I'd do your grandmother a favour," whispered the Tall Man. His skin was as white as the plaster ceiling. "You were busy with your book, and your grandmother looked so tired tonight. . . ."

The Tall Men always brought bad news. Was

there something wrong now with grandmother? Charlotte ran past the man and dashed into her grandmother's room. The old woman was already in bed, pulling the blanket up over her shoulders. "Charlotte! What's wrong?" she asked.

"The man . . ." Charlotte could hardly breathe.

"What man?"

Charlotte could hear her heart beating. "The man in the kitchen."

Her grandmother was out of bed at once. She walked swiftly to the kitchen with Charlotte following.

"There's no one here," said the old woman. "You must have fallen asleep and had a dream."

Charlotte was confused, but glad that the man was gone. And that her grandmother was strong and healthy. The Tall Man certainly hadn't come for the old woman, standing there firmly in the middle of the room.

Charlotte heard a bark outside. That was her dog. Not the thing that had turned into the Tall Man. *Her* dog. Charlotte ran to the door, pulled it open and yelled, "Kenji! Kenji!"

The dog, who always answered with a bark once the back door was open, was not in the garden.

"Kenji!"

Charlotte ran towards the street. She heard a car screeching its brakes nearby, then a dog's loud yelp. Then nothing.

She saw the shadow of a man standing at the end of the block. A tall, tall man.

THE GIRL IN THE GRAVEYARD

A cold breeze blew in Bradley's face as he steered his bicycle into the old graveyard. Falling leaves, their edges sharp and dry, seemed to bite at his cheeks and his bare hands. It was almost as if the wind knew something that day. As if the air itself, the dark October air that lay huddled around the cemetery's headstones, was trying to stop the boy. It gusted against the tyres and frame. It seemed as though it was warning him to take another way.

"Hey, kid! Look out!" yelled a college student who was busy raking leaves in the graveyard. Bradley, without thinking, cycled right through the pile. *Whoosh!* "Sorry," Bradley yelled back over his shoulder.

"Sorry isn't good enough!" the student shouted, raking more furiously than before.

Bradley grinned as he gripped the handlebars and kept his eyes straight ahead. He had never taken this shortcut home before. There were a lot of headstones to avoid and the wind was strong. He followed the well-worn paths that led around old trees and beside rows of waving bushes. He pedalled past statues of weeping angels whose faces had been worn away by weather and time. The narrow path led Bradley near a small, spooky building that looked like an ancient temple he'd seen in his history textbook.

"Boo!"

A strange girl, her head cloaked in scarves and a cap, jumped out from behind the building and lunged at Bradley. The startled boy swerved, almost crashing into a tree. He stopped his bike and could hear the girl giggling behind him. He turned as he shouted, "That's not funny!"

The girl had gone.

Bradley leaned his bike against the tree and quickly walked around the small temple. He thought the girl might be hiding there. When he found that he was alone, Bradley climbed back on his bike and headed down the trail.

He had only been cycling for a few seconds when the girl jumped out from behind a headstone. She flapped her arms at him, then ran off. Bradley shot after her, but he quickly lost her among the rows and rows of gravestones and the growing dusk.

Angry, he turned back to the path.

With each minute, the sun sank lower behind the trees. More leaves drifted from the branches. The cold wind blew them towards Bradley's bike, where they swirled and then vanished behind his humming tyres.

Twice more the strange girl jumped out at him, trying to scare him. Bradley kept his mouth firmly shut and tried his best to ignore her. He would merely swerve out of the way, turn his face from her, and keep pedaling.

Bradley could see the long wall that marked the west side of the graveyard. Beyond that wall was the street that led to his home. It had been several minutes and the girl had not reappeared. *Maybe she's finished with her stupid game,* he thought. Whoever she was. Was she the little sister of the college kid that was raking leaves? Bradley didn't care. His attention was on the brick wall that lay up ahead.

Although . . .

Something about the strange girl bothered him. Not the fact that she had been annoying him this whole time. It was her appearance.

She was bundled up in a swirl of scarves and a long blue coat. She wore a tight knit cap pulled down over her hair. Bradley hadn't seen her face. It had been hidden deep within the folds of her scarves, or hidden by the shadow of a nearby tree or statue. Yet the girl looked familiar.

The blue coat. The scarves. And whenever the girl ran away or waved her arms at him, she moved awkwardly. Stiffly. As if it were hard for her to bend her knees and elbows. Like an action figure. Or a –

Bradley stopped his bike. In the deepening gloom, he saw the shadow of the girl moving against the dark brick wall up ahead. She was walking jerkily, like a robot. Back and forth, back and forth.

Like a doll.

Two days ago, Bradley had pulled a prank on his twin sister, Daisy. He had taken one of her dolls and would only give it back if Daisy gave him all her snacks for a month. If their mum baked biscuits, for example, Bradley would be able to eat his sister's share along with his own. Daisy had reluctantly agreed in order to get her doll back. But when Bradley returned the doll, its face was missing. He had hidden the toy behind a heater in the basement, and the doll's face had melted away, leaving only a strange, smooth mess in its place.

Bradley insisted he hadn't done it on purpose, but he was still punished. "For your carelessness," his mother had said. Bradley had been grounded for a month. Which was one of the reasons he had taken the shortcut through the graveyard – to get home quickly, before his new curfew began.

It was getting late. The girl was still walking back and forth in front of the wall. The wind was getting stronger, colder, but Bradley was sweating. He remembered how the doll was dressed. In a long blue coat and a bunch of scarves wrapped around its melted head.

The girl stopped walking. She turned and stared at Bradley.

The boy's anger returned. He wasn't going to let this bother him anymore. He wasn't going to be tricked by some bratty kid, some annoying friend of his sister's. Bradley pedalled towards the wall.

He braked a metre from the strange girl. "Forget it," he said boldly. "I know who you are. I know why you're doing this."

It was dark within the lengthening shadow of the wall. The girl stood still. The wind tugged at the scarves hiding her face.

Bradley wondered what her expression would be. Fear? Surprise?

"You can tell Daisy it didn't work," Bradley said.

The girl stepped closer. The wind blew harder. One of the scarves came undone and fluttered down to her feet. Now Bradley could see that from the brow of her knit cap down to the scarves, she had no expression at all. The girl had no eyes, no nose, no mouth. A flat, melted smoothness was all that showed.

Bradley cried out as the girl reached her stiff robotic arms towards him and his bike. He felt the sweat pouring down his neck, his face. And then one of his eyes slid down his chin, and then his nose. And then . . . it all went blank.

ABOUT THE AUTHOR

Michael Dahl, the author of the Library of Doom and Troll Hunters series, is an expert on fear. He is afraid of heights (but he still flies). He is afraid of small, enclosed spaces (but his house is crammed with over 3000 books). He is afraid of ghosts (but that same house is haunted). He hopes that by writing about fear, he will eventually be able to overcome his own. So far it is not working. But he is afraid to stop. He claims that, if he had to, he would travel to Mount Doom in order to throw in a dangerous piece of jewellery. Even though he is afraid of volcanoes. And jewellery.

ABOUT THE ILLUSTRATOR

Xavier Bonet is an illustrator and comic-book artist who resides in Barcelona. Experienced in 2D illustration, he has worked as an animator and a background artist for several different production companies. He aims to create works full of colour, texture and sensation, using both traditional and digital tools. His work in children's literature is inspired by magic and fantasy as well as his passion for art.

MICHAEL DAHL TELLS ALL

Scary stories are fun to write. It's a way for me to get my fears out in the open, give them a voice, shine a light on them and hopefully watch them dwindle away in the spotlight. Ideas for scary stories start with you. What are you afraid of? What really terrifies you? Make a list, write them down. And voilà, you have a table of contents for a book of eerie tales.

LITTLE IMPS

Mirrors fascinate me. After I read *Alice Through the Looking Glass* when I was nine years old, I tried climbing through various mirrors in my house. Just so you know, it didn't work. Despite my failures, I was sure there was another world on the other side. I still am sure; the trick is how to get there. This tale, besides tying in my thing for mirrors, also includes a term thrown at my childhood friends and me by some of the neighbourhood grown-ups. "Little imps!" We were too noisy, too boisterous and having too much fun. But "imp" has another meaning, as the sisters discover in this story.

NIGHT OF THE FALLING STAR

My mother saw a meteor one morning. She saw it crash in the field beyond the train tracks that bordered our garden. She said it had colourful lights all around its edge too. My friends and I knew what it really was. A UFO! That afternoon, we walked across the tracks and investigated the field. No meteor, but we did find a large round imprint in the ground. Grass grew around the edges of it, but nothing grew inside. What had my mother really seen that morning? Ever since then, I've wanted to write a story about children who encounter a meteor. But would the rock from outer space be radioactive? Would it have a weird effect on people who got too close? Maybe it's a good thing my friends and I didn't find anything on the other side of the tracks.

THE BABY MONITOR

This is one of those ideas that just popped into my head when I saw a picture of a baby monitor online. What if the baby monitor was actually a baby? Babies are scary creatures. They crawl, they slobber, they eat whatever they find lying around and they scream. That could easily describe an alien monster. Later, I dreamed a baby was walking towards my bedroom in the middle of the night. I woke up, totally creeped out, wrote it all down in a notepad and finished the story the next day.

THE HUNGRY SNOWMAN

I read a lot of science fiction (sci-fi), including old sci-fi comics. One of the comics I've collected has an outrageously bonkers cover. It shows evil alien snowmen invading Earth, shooting death rays from their eyes. So cool. I happened to see this one again while hunting for something to read, and it got me thinking. Not all snowmen are Frosty. And if a snowman did come to life, what would it eat? Something that's easy to reach, I thought, something close at hand!

THE TALL AND SLENDER MAN

This is my addition to the Slender Man urban legend. I decided to make him the messenger of bad news. Whether he causes bad things to happen, or simply warns people about them is left up in the air. You as a reader can decide. I have a friend with a pup called Kenji, so that's where the dog's name came from.

THE GIRL IN THE GRAVEYARD

What goes around comes around. Karma. Do something good and it will come back to you. But do something bad . . . look out! That's the point of this story. A bad deed, even something minor like pranking a sister or a friend, will create another bad deed that will bounce back at you. I thought a graveyard would be the perfect setting for Bradley to meet his destiny. A destiny that involves an unliving person. I say "unliving" because dolls, strictly speaking, aren't dead, as they're not alive in the first place. Or are they?

GLOSSARY

biology study of life and all living things

carelessness failure to pay attention

expression look on someone's face that shows what he or she is thinking or feeling

furiously fiercely or angrily

gravestone piece of carved rock that marks someone's burial site

hind at the back or rear

icicle ice formation caused by water that freezes as it drips

imp small child who is full of mischief, or an evil spirit

meteor piece of rock or metal that speeds into Earth's atmosphere from space and forms a streak of light as it burns and falls to Earth

omen sign or warning about your luck in the future

ooze flow or seep out slowly

static electrical discharges in the air that interfere with radio or television signals and cause a hissing or crackling sound

swerve turn suddenly while moving forward

vegetarian person who doesn't eat meat

DISCUSSION QUESTIONS

1. Can you explain why Eddie and Ollie shrank in "Night of the Falling Star"? What details in the story support your explanation?

2. In the story "The Tall and Slender Man", Charlotte reads about Tall Men, who are omens – or signs of things (usually bad things) to come. Can you think of any omens you've heard of or seen in your life?

3. Who is the main character in "The Hungry Snowman"? How do you know? Discuss using examples from the text.

WRITING PROMPTS

1. In the story "Little Imps", Hattie meets a monster with pink, scaly skin and yellow cat's eyes in her bathroom. Do you think the monster is her sister, Isabel? Explain why or why not using examples from the story.

2. Bradley takes a shortcut through the cemetery in "The Girl in the Graveyard". Imagine you're the girl watching him pedal by, and write the scene from her perspective.

3. When "The Baby Monitor" ends, Samantha Moore is missing and her mother has packed the monitor away in the basement. Write a story in which someone comes across the monitor and hears Samantha's voice coming from the other end.

MICHAEL DAHL'S
REALLY SCARY STORIES